Sarah's Grandma Goes to Heaven

Written by Maribeth Boelts

Illustrated by Cheri Bladholm

Zonderkidz

Zonder**kidz**.

The children's group of Zondervan

www.zonderkidz.com

Sarah's Grandma Goes to Heaven
Copyright © 2004 by The Zondervan Corporation
Illustrations copyright © 2004 by Cheri Bladholm

Requests for information should be addressed to:
Zonderkidz, *Grand Rapids, Michigan 49530*

Library of Congress Cataloging-in-Publication Data

Boelts, Maribeth, 1964-
    Sarah's Grandma goes to heaven : a book about grief / by Maribeth Boelts.–1st ed.
        p. cm. – (Helping kids heal)
    Summary: A young girl comes to understand more about death, funerals, and heaven when her
beloved grandmother dies of cancer.
    ISBN 0-310-70656-4 (Hardcover)
    [1. Death — Fiction. 2. Grief — Fiction. 3. Grandmothers — Fiction. 4. Christian life — Fiction.]
I. Title. II. Series.
    PZ7.B6338Sar 2004
    [E]– dc22

                                                        2003021479

Editor: Gwen Ellis
Art Direction & Design: Laura M. Maitner

Printed in China

---

05 06 07/ HK /4 3 2

In Loving Memory
of Carolyn Hau
Maribeth Boelts

To Grandpa Dan and Grammy Gloria, Hannah,
Holly, and Patrick for modeling for this book and
sparkling with His strong, pure, light.
Cheri Bladholm

GRANDMA AND SARAH picked green beans as the summer sun heated the soft dirt between Sarah's toes.

"Can we go to the pool after lunch, Grandma?" Sarah asked.

"Maybe..." said Grandma. "But Grandpa will need to take you because I have a doctor appointment."

"Are you sick?" Sarah asked.

"I'm not sure," Grandma said. "I just haven't been feeling like myself lately."

A few days later, Mom and Dad had a talk with Sarah.

Mom held her hand and told her that Grandma was sick with a disease called cancer. She would need special medicine and many visits to the doctor.

"Will she die?" Sarah asked, her heart pounding.

"Some people who get cancer or are sick in other ways get well again," said Dad. "We don't know what will happen in Grandma's case. We're taking one day at a time and praying that she will get better."

Soon the leaves lit the streets in orange and red, and the pumpkins in the garden were ready to harvest. Grandma sat in a deck chair while Sarah rolled the giant pumpkins until they made an orange circle around her chair. Together, they scooped and carved until there was a pumpkin family.

Grandma's soft, white hair had fallen out from the medicine she was taking so Sarah had given her a favorite baseball cap to cover her head. When she finished carving Grandma's pumpkin, Sarah ran in the house to get another cap for the pumpkin to wear. Grandma laughed and said, "Why, that looks just like me, Sarah!"

BEFORE CHRISTMAS, Grandma grew sicker. A nurse named Amy started coming during the day, and Mom and Dad took turns staying with Grandma, too.

As Grandpa held the cookie sheet close to her wheelchair, Grandma sprinkled cookies with red and green sugar. In a weak voice, she read Sarah the Christmas story and let Sarah put Baby Jesus in the manger. Later, when Grandma napped, Sarah knelt by the stable. She held Baby Jesus in her hand. She prayed that Grandma would get well and be able to play with her and work in her garden again.

BUT IN JANUARY, as the winter winds blew…Grandma died.

Suddenly, there were family and friends visiting. The kitchen table filled up with relatives who cried and laughed and shared stories about Grandma. Sarah was hugged and hugged again and offered sandwiches and brownies, but it was hard to be hungry.

Snow fell that day, and so did Grandpa's tears. Sarah sat with him in the rocking chair, and they talked about how much Grandma loved God, her family, and her garden. They talked about heaven, and Grandpa told Sarah that in heaven there is no sickness, or crying, or sadness.

"Will we see Grandma again?" she asked.

"Someday we will," Grandpa said. "When we go to heaven."

"When will that be?" asked Sarah.

"When we die," Grandpa said.

Sarah was quiet. "Will I be very old when I die?"

Grandpa rested his hand on Sarah's head. "Most people are, Sarah."

THAT NIGHT, Mom asked Sarah if she would like to go to Grandma's funeral. She explained that Grandma's body would be there in a casket, but her spirit would be in heaven with Jesus. She said that some people would be crying and some people would be sitting quietly while the pastor talked. They would sing songs and tell stories about Grandma's life.

"I want to go," said Sarah. So Mom helped her choose her clothes for the funeral. Aunt Meg thought Sarah should wear her best dress and her black, shiny shoes. Aunt Meg didn't know that the shoes pinched Sarah's feet and her best dress was itchy.

"Grandma would want you to be comfortable, wouldn't she?" Mom said later. Sarah chose her white sneakers, a blouse, and a jumper that Grandma had sewn a new button on.

Sarah showed Mom the button.

"I miss her," Sarah said. She gulped hard.

"Me too," said Mom, as she drew Sarah close.

AT BEDTIME Sarah couldn't sleep, so Mom and Dad let her climb in with them.

Sarah talked about Grandma for a long time. Then Dad read Grandma's favorite part of the Bible out loud, and Sarah listened as Dad's words described the Lord as a shepherd. Sarah closed her eyes and imagined the still waters and lying down in green pastures.

"Can I draw a picture of that?" Sarah asked.

While Dad read the passage again, Sarah drew a picture of a shepherd and a green field and still water, but instead of a sheep, she drew a picture of Grandma with soft white hair, and her face smiling.

AT THE FUNERAL, Sarah slowly walked to where Grandma's body lay in the casket. At first, it was scary.

"Is she sleeping?" Sarah asked.

"When people die, they aren't sleeping," Dad said quietly. "Their bodies don't breathe, think, feel, or hear anymore."

Sarah stood still and thought about Grandma's body in the casket and Grandma's spirit in heaven.

"How do you know Grandma is in heaven?" Sarah asked.

"Because she loved God, and believed in his Son, Jesus," said Dad. "God said that if we do those two things, we'll go to heaven to be with him. It's a promise God makes."

Sarah reached in her jumper pocket for the drawing she had made the night before. She laid it on Grandma's folded hands.

"I'll see you again, Grandma," Sarah said.

A FEW DAYS AFTER THE FUNERAL, Grandpa called and asked if Sarah would like to come over. So all that winter as snow turned to spring rain, Sarah and Grandpa played checkers, ordered hot chocolate at the restaurant downtown, and built block cities that filled half the living room floor. Some days, Grandpa's eyes were tired, and when he talked about Grandma, his voice sounded like he wanted to cry. And some days they laughed about a good joke Sarah had heard, or a funny story about Grandma.

A FEW DAYS AFTER THE FUNERAL, Grandpa called and asked if Sarah would like to come over. So all that winter as snow turned to spring rain, Sarah and Grandpa played checkers, ordered hot chocolate at the restaurant downtown, and built block cities that filled half the living room floor. Some days, Grandpa's eyes were tired, and when he talked about Grandma, his voice sounded like he wanted to cry. And some days they laughed about a good joke Sarah had heard, or a funny story about Grandma.

WHEN THE PUDDLES dried and the days grew warm, Grandpa and Sarah started digging in the garden. They planted green beans, rows of corn, and buried tiny mounds of pumpkin seeds. And just like the pasture Dad had read about in the Bible, soon everywhere Sarah looked she saw green and growing things.

"Grandma would have loved this garden," Sarah said.

"You're right," said Grandpa. "But do you know what she would have loved best of all?"

"What?" asked Sarah.

Grandpa put his arm around Sarah's shoulder. "She would have loved the gardeners."

And Sarah, remembering the love her grandma had shown her every day, agreed.

We want you to know what happens to those who die.

We don't want you to be sad, as other people are.

They don't have any hope. We believe that Jesus died

and rose again. When he returns…God will bring them

[those who have died] back with Jesus

(1 Thessalonians 4:13–14).

When Someone Close to Your Child Dies

Death is a difficult subject for any parent to face with a child. The passing of a grandparent is frequently a child's first encounter with death. Very young children have a difficult time grasping the reality and finality of death. No matter what age your child may be, when the subject of the death of someone close to them comes up, he or she needs reassurance.

Sufficient reassurance can keep the child from feeling helpless and hopeless in the face of loss.

- Reassure your child that death is a part of life, and it is not the end for Christians.
- Reassure your child that God is with him or her *no matter what happens.* This is a truth that has comforted God's people throughout the generations.
- Reassure the child that he or she is safe.
- Reassure your child that you are safe.

One way to get this point across is to say something like, "I hope you know that even though Grandma died, I'm not leaving, and neither are you. We'll be around each other for a *very* long time! Maybe right now we need to spend some extra time with each other." Being together is a precious gift at any time, but in this situation, it is a very real comfort and an important way to cope with loss.

You give your child a wonderful gift when you let him or her see your openness in facing death. So don't be afraid to show your emotions to your child. You may feel like crying as you read this book. Go ahead. It's all right to be upset and cry in front of your child. Part of giving your child permission to grieve is letting your child know that you are grieving, too. Grief and sadness are important emotions, and this loss is a special experience you can share.

In this book, Sarah and her grandfather share some special memories of Grandma. It helps to have a special activity that reminds the child of the person who died. Sometimes it's a special celebration. Sometimes it's an activity your child did with that person—such as camping or canning peaches. Sometimes it's recalling memories of certain holidays or keeping a holiday tradition alive. Sometimes it's going through old pictures, movies, videos, or making a memory scrapbook. Make plans with your child to do something like this *and then do it*. Thinking about and celebrating the life of your loved one is often more valuable than visiting a burial site.

Talk with your child about the ways you are reminded that God is with you. Maybe it's in a sunset, in the changing seasons, in a special Bible verse, in an everyday event. Encourage your child to think about how he or she is reminded that God is there. Talk about this from time to time.

Just the fact that you read this book to your child can help the child understand he or she is not alone. You are there. God is there. Read and reread this book as a reminder and a reassurance of this wonderful truth.

A Word to Parents and Other Caregivers

Everyday life in God's world presents challenges and problems for all of us. Children, as well as adults, struggle with a variety of feelings when faced with emotionally charged situations. By helping our children clearly recognize God's loving presence in their lives—that he is with them no matter what happens—we help to prepare them for life. One of the names of Jesus Christ is "Emanuel, God with us," and God with us is the pervasive theme of this Helping Kids Heal series. The books honestly and sensitively address the difficult emotions children face.

Children love a good story, and stories can provide a safe way to approach issues, concerns, and problems. Therapists who work with children have long used stories to help children acknowledge emotions they would rather avoid. When a loving parent, a kind grandparent, or a caring teacher reads about a story character who is experiencing difficult feelings, the child has permission to feel, to ask questions, to voice his or her fears, and to struggle with emotions. Remember, as with any good story, one reading is never enough. Repetition is a great reminder of the truths contained in the story.

Each child is different. Some children, when facing a difficult emotion, will ask questions and wonder aloud about the characters in the books. Other children are content to just listen and take it all in. After several readings, try to draw them out to talk about the story. You, more than anyone else, will know what the child needs. Keep these things in mind as you use these books:

- God is with you, too. You may be reading about something that is close to your heart. Your emotions may be as tender as the child's as you read the story. Pray that you will have a sense of God's loving presence in your heart.

- You do not have to know the perfect answer for every question, nor do you have to answer all of the child's questions. Some of the best questions are the hardest to answer. Be sure, however, to acknowledge the child's question. Be honest. Say that you don't have the answer. If the child asks, "Why did she have to die?" it's all right to say, "I don't know."

- Pray with the child to feel God's loving presence. Let the child know that you care about him or her and about his or her feelings. Let the child know that whether he or she feels God's presence or not, God is still with him or her. This is a loving, precious, and powerful gift that you can give the child.

- Be aware that God works in a variety of ways. You may not get much of a response from the child as you read this book. Don't be concerned. Read the book at different times. You are planting a seed—a seed for the child to recognize God is at work in everyone's life.

- Have fun! Enjoy the story and this time with the child. Children are precious gifts from God created in his image. God is helping you to prepare the child for a future in his kingdom.

Dr. Scott

R. Scott Stehouwer, Ph.D., professor of psychology, Calvin College, and clinical psychologist